Fyodor Dostoyevsky

An Unpleasant Predicament: A Nasty Story
(Unabridged)

e-artnow 2019

Fyodor Dostoyevsky

An Unpleasant Predicament: A Nasty Story
(Unabridged)

Translated by Constance Garnett

e-artnow, 2018
Contact: info@e-artnow.org
ISBN 978-80-273-3365-3

An Unpleasant Predicament (A Nasty Story)

This unpleasant business occurred at the epoch when the regeneration of our beloved father-land and the struggle of her valiant sons towards new hopes and destinies was beginning with irresistible force and with a touchingly naïve impetuosity. One winter evening in that period, between eleven and twelve o'clock, three highly respectable gentlemen were sitting in a comfort-able and even luxuriously furnished room in a handsome house of two storeys on the Petersburg Side, and were engaged in a staid and edifying conversation on a very interesting subject. These three gentlemen were all of generals' rank. They were sitting round a little table, each in a soft and handsome armchair, and as they talked, they quietly and luxuriously sipped champagne. The bottle stood on the table on a silver stand with ice round it. The fact was that the host, a privy councillor called Stepan Nikiforovitch Nikiforov, an old bachelor of sixty-five, was cele-brating his removal into a house he had just bought, and as it happened, also his birthday, which he had never kept before. The festivity, however, was not on a very grand scale; as we have seen already, there were only two guests, both of them former colleagues and former subordinates of Mr. Nikiforov; that is, an actual civil councillor called Semyon Ivanovitch Shipulenko, and another actual civil councillor, Ivan Ilyitch Pralinsky. They had arrived to tea at nine o'clock, then had begun upon the wine, and knew that at exactly half-past eleven they would have to set off home. Their host had all his life been fond of regularity. A few words about him.

He had begun his career as a petty clerk with nothing to back him, had quietly plodded on for forty-five years, knew very well what to work towards, had no ambition to draw the stars down from heaven, though he had two stars already, and particularly disliked expressing his own opinion on any subject. He was honest, too, that is, it had not happened to him to do anything particularly dishonest; he was a bachelor because he was an egoist; he had plenty of brains, but he could not bear showing his intelligence; he particularly disliked slovenliness and enthusi-asm, regarding it as moral slovenliness; and towards the end of his life had become completely absorbed in a voluptuous, indolent comfort and systematic solitude. Though he sometimes vis-ited people of a rather higher rank than his own, yet from his youth up he could never endure entertaining visitors himself; and of late he had, if he did not play a game of patience, been satisfied with the society of his dining-room clock, and would spend the whole evening dozing in his armchair, listening placidly to its ticking under its glass case on the chimney-piece. In appearance he was closely shaven and extremely proper-looking, he was well-preserved, looking younger than his age; he promised to go on living many years longer, and closely followed the rules of the highest good breeding. His post was a fairly comfortable one: he had to preside somewhere and to sign something. In short, he was regarded as a first-rate man. He had only one passion, or more accurately, one keen desire: that was, to have his own house, and a house built like a gentleman's residence, not a commercial investment. His desire was at last realised: he looked out and bought a house on the Petersburg Side, a good way off, it is true, but it had a garden and was an elegant house. The new owner decided that it was better for being a good way off: he did not like entertaining at home, and for driving to see any one or to the office he had a handsome carriage of a chocolate hue, a coachman, Mihey, and two little but strong and handsome horses. All this was honourably acquired by the careful frugality of forty years, so that his heart rejoiced over it.

This was how it was that Stepan Nikiforovitch felt such pleasure in his placid heart that he actually invited two friends to see him on his birthday, which he had hitherto carefully concealed from his most intimate acquaintances. He had special designs on one of these visi-tors. He lived in the upper storey of his new house, and he wanted a tenant for the lower half, which was built and arranged in exactly the same way. Stepan Nikiforovitch was reckoning upon Semyon Ivanovitch Shipulenko, and had twice that evening broached the subject in the course of conversation. But Semyon Ivanovitch made no response. The latter, too, was a man who had doggedly made a way for himself in the course of long years. He had black hair and whiskers, and a face that always had a shade of jaundice. He was a married man of morose disposition who liked to stay at home; he ruled his household with a rod of iron; in his official duties he had the greatest self-confidence. He, too, knew perfectly well what goal he was making for, and better still, what he never would reach. He was in a good position, and he was sitting tight there. Though he looked upon the new reforms with a certain distaste, he was not particularly agitated about them: he was extremely self-confident, and listened with a shade of ironical malice to Ivan Ilyitch Pralinsky expatiating on new themes. All of them had been drinking rather freely, however, so that Stepan Nikiforovitch himself condescended to take part in a slight discussion with Mr. Pralinsky concerning the latest reforms. But we must say a few words about his Excellency, Mr. Pralinsky, especially as he is the chief hero of the present story.

The actual civil councillor Ivan Ilyitch Pralinsky had only been "his Excellency" for four months; in short, he was a young general. He was young in years, too — only forty-three, no more — and he looked and liked to look even younger. He was a tall, handsome man, he was smart in his dress, and prided himself on its solid, dignified character; with great aplomb he displayed an order of some consequence on his breast. From his earliest childhood he had known how to acquire the airs and graces of aristocratic society, and being a bachelor, dreamed of a wealthy and even aristocratic bride. He dreamed of many other things, though he was far from being stupid. At times he was a great talker, and even liked to assume a parliamentary pose. He came of a good family. He was the son of a general, and brought up in the lap of luxury; in his tender childhood he had been dressed in velvet and fine linen, had been educated at an aristocratic school, and though he acquired very little learning there he was successful in the service, and had worked his way up to being a general. The authorities looked upon him as a capable man, and even expected great things from him in the future. Stepan Nikiforovitch, under whom Ivan Ilyitch had begun his career in the service, and under whom he had remained until he was made a general, had never considered him a good business man and had no expectations of him whatever. What he liked in him was that he belonged to a good family, had property — that is, a big block of buildings, let out in flats, in charge of an overseer — was connected with persons of consequence, and what was more, had a majestic bearing. Stepan Nikiforovitch blamed him inwardly for excess of imagination and instability. Ivan Ilyitch himself felt at times that he had too much *amour-propre* and even sensitiveness. Strange to say, he had attacks from time to time of morbid tenderness of conscience and even a kind of faint remorse. With bitterness and a secret soreness of heart he recognised now and again that he did not fly so high as he imagined. At such moments he sank into despondency, especially when he was suffering from hæmorrhoids, called his life *une existence manquée*, and ceased — privately, of course — to believe even in his parliamentary capacities, calling himself a talker, a maker of phrases; and though all that, of course, did him great credit, it did not in the least prevent him from raising his head again half an hour later, and growing even more obstinately, even more conceitedly self-confident, and assuring himself that he would yet succeed in making his mark, and that he would be not only a great official, but a statesman whom Russia would long remember. He actually dreamed at times of monuments. From this it will be seen that Ivan Ilyitch aimed high, though he hid his vague hopes and dreams deep in his heart, even with a certain trepidation. In short, he was a goodnatured man and a poet at heart. Of late years these morbid moments of disillusionment had begun to be more frequent. He had become peculiarly irritable, ready to take offence, and was apt to take any contradiction as an affront. But reformed Russia gave him great hopes. His promotion to general was the finishing touch. He was roused; he held his head up. He suddenly began talking freely and eloquently. He talked about the new ideas, which he very quickly and unexpectedly made his own and professed with vehemence. He sought opportunities for speaking, drove about the town, and in many places succeeded in gaining the reputation of a desperate Liberal, which flattered him greatly. That evening, after drinking four glasses, he was particularly exuberant. He wanted on every point to confute Stepan Nikiforovitch, whom he had not seen for some time past, and whom he had hitherto always respected and even obeyed. He considered him for some reason reactionary, and fell upon him with exceptional heat. Stepan Nikiforovitch hardly answered him, but only listened slyly, though the subject interested him. Ivan Ilyitch got hot, and in the heat of the discussion sipped his glass more often than he ought to have done. Then Stepan Nikiforovitch took the bottle and at once filled his glass again, which for some reason seemed to offend Ivan Ilyitch, especially as Semyon Ivanovitch Shipulenko, whom he particularly despised and indeed feared on account of his cynicism and ill-nature, preserved a treacherous silence and smiled more frequently than was necessary. "They seem to take me for a schoolboy," flashed across Ivan Ilyitch's mind.

"No, it was time, high time," he went on hotly. "We have put it off too long, and to my thinking humanity is the first consideration, humanity with our inferiors, remembering that they, too, are men. Humanity will save everything and bring out all that is...."

"He-he-he-he!" was heard from the direction of Semyon Ivanovitch.

"But why are you giving us such a talking to?" Stepan Nikiforovitch protested at last, with an affable smile. "I must own, Ivan Ilyitch, I have not been able to make out, so far, what you are maintaining. You advocate humanity. That is love of your fellow-creatures, isn't it?"

"Yes, if you like. I...."

"Allow me! As far as I can see, that's not the only thing. Love of one's fellow-creatures has always been fitting. The reform movement is not confined to that. All sorts of questions have arisen relating to the peasantry, the law courts, economics, government contracts, morals and... and...and those questions are endless, and all together may give rise to great upheavals, so to say. That is what we have been anxious about, and not simply humanity...."

"Yes, the thing is a bit deeper than that," observed Semyon Ivanovitch.

"I quite understand, and allow me to observe, Semyon Ivanovitch, that I can't agree to being inferior to you in depth of understanding," Ivan Ilyitch observed sarcastically and with excessive sharpness. "However, I will make so bold as to assert, Stepan Nikiforovitch, that you have not understood me either...."

"No, I haven't."

"And yet I maintain and everywhere advance the idea that humanity and nothing else with one's subordinates, from the official in one's department down to the copying clerk, from the copying clerk down to the house serf, from the servant down to the peasant — humanity, I say, may serve, so to speak, as the cornerstone of the coming reforms and the reformation of things in general. Why? Because. Take a syllogism. I am human, consequently I am loved. I am loved, so confidence is felt in me. There is a feeling of confidence, and so there is trust. There is trust, and so there is love...that is, no, I mean to say that if they trust me they will believe in the reforms, they will understand, so to speak, the essential nature of them, will, so to speak, embrace each other in a moral sense, and will settle the whole business in a friendly way, fundamentally. What are you laughing at, Semyon Ivanovitch? Can't you understand?"

Stepan Nikiforovitch raised his eyebrows without speaking; he was surprised.

"I fancy I have drunk a little too much," said Semyon Ivanovitch sarcastically, "and so I am a little slow of comprehension. Not quite all my wits about me."

Ivan Ilyitch winced.

"We should break down," Stepan Nikiforovitch pronounced suddenly, after a slight pause of hesitation.

"How do you mean we should break down?" asked Ivan Ilyitch, surprised at Stepan Nikiforovitch's abrupt remark.

"Why, we should break under the strain." Stepan Nikiforovitch evidently did not care to explain further.

"I suppose you are thinking of new wine in old bottles?" Ivan Ilyitch replied, not without irony. "Well, I can answer for myself, anyway."

At that moment the clock struck half-past eleven.

"One sits on and on, but one must go at last," said Semyon Ivanovitch, getting up. But Ivan Ilyitch was before him; he got up from the table and took his sable cap from the chimney-piece. He looked as though he had been insulted.

"So how is it to be, Semyon Ivanovitch? Will you think it over?" said Stepan Nikiforovitch, as he saw the visitors out.

"About the flat, you mean? I'll think it over, I'll think it over."

"Well, when you have made up your mind, let me know as soon as possible."

"Still on business?" Mr. Pralinsky observed affably, in a slightly ingratiating tone, playing with his hat. It seemed to him as though they were forgetting him.

Stepan Nikiforovitch raised his eyebrows and remained mute, as a sign that he would not detain his visitors. Semyon Ivanovitch made haste to bow himself out.

"Well... after that what is one to expect... if you don't understand the simple rules of good manners...." Mr. Pralinsky reflected to himself, and held out his hand to Stepan Nikiforovitch in a particularly offhand way.

In the hall Ivan Ilyitch wrapped himself up in his light, expensive fur coat; he tried for some reason not to notice Semyon Ivanovitch's shabby raccoon, and they both began descending the stairs.

"The old man seemed offended," said Ivan Ilyitch to the silent Semyon Ivanovitch.

"No, why?" answered the latter with cool composure.

"Servile flunkey," Ivan Ilyitch thought to himself.

They went out at the front door. Semyon Ivanovitch's sledge with a grey ugly horse drove up.

"What the devil! What has Trifon done with my carriage?" cried Ivan Ilyitch, not seeing his carriage.

The carriage was nowhere to be seen. Stepan Nikiforovitch's servant knew nothing about it. They appealed to Varlam, Semyon Ivanovitch's coachman, and received the answer that he had been standing there all the time and that the carriage had been there, but now there was no sign of it.

"An unpleasant predicament," Mr. Shipulenko pronounced. "Shall I take you home?"

"Scoundrelly people!" Mr. Pralinsky cried with fury. "He asked me, the rascal, to let him go to a wedding close here in the Petersburg Side; some crony of his was getting married, deuce take her! I sternly forbade him to absent himself, and now I'll bet he has gone off there."

"He certainly has gone there, sir," observed Varlam; "but he promised to be back in a minute, to be here in time, that is."

"Well, there it is! I had a presentiment that this would happen! I'll give it to him!"

"You'd better give him a good flogging once or twice at the police station, then he will do what you tell him," said Semyon Ivanovitch, as he wrapped the rug round him.

"Please don't you trouble, Semyon Ivanovitch!"

"Well, won't you let me take you along?"

"*Merci, bon voyage.*"

Semyon Ivanovitch drove off, while Ivan Ilyitch set off on foot along the wooden pavement, conscious of a rather acute irritation.

"Yes, indeed I'll give it to you now, you rogue! I am going on foot on purpose to make you feel it, to frighten you! He will come back and hear that his master has gone off on foot... the blackguard!"

Ivan Ilyitch had never abused any one like this, but he was greatly angered, and besides, there was a buzzing in his head. He was not given to drink, so five or six glasses soon affected him. But the night was enchanting. There was a frost, but it was remarkably still and there was no wind. There was a clear, starry sky. The full moon was bathing the earth in soft silver light. It was so lovely that after walking some fifty paces Ivan Ilyitch almost forgot his troubles. He felt particularly pleased. People quickly change from one mood to another when they are a little drunk. He was even pleased with the ugly little wooden houses of the deserted street.

"It's really a capital thing that I am walking," he thought; "it's a lesson to Trifon and a pleasure to me. I really ought to walk oftener. And I shall soon pick up a sledge on the Great Prospect. It's a glorious night. What little houses they all are! I suppose small fry live here, clerks, tradesmen, perhaps.... That Stepan Nikiforovitch! What reactionaries they all are, those old fogies! Fogies, yes, *c'est le mot*. He is a sensible man, though; he has that *bon sens*, sober, practical understanding of things. But they are old, old. There is a lack of...what is it? There is a lack of something.... 'We shall break down.' What did he mean by that? He actually pondered when he said it. He didn't understand me a bit. And yet how could he help understanding? It was more difficult not to understand it than to understand it. The chief thing is that I am convinced, convinced in my soul. Humanity... the love of one's kind. Restore a man to himself, revive his personal dignity, and then...when the ground is prepared, get to work. I believe that's clear? Yes! Allow me, your Excellency; take a syllogism, for instance: we meet, for instance, a clerk, a poor, downtrodden clerk. 'Well...who are you?' Answer: 'A clerk.' Very good, a clerk; further: 'What sort of clerk are you?' Answer: 'I am such and such a clerk,' he says. 'Are you in the service?' 'I am.' 'Do you want to be happy?' 'I do.' 'What do you need for happiness?' 'This and that.' 'Why?' 'Because....' and there the man understands me with a couple of words, the man's mine, the man is caught, so to speak, in a net, and I can do what I like with him, that is, for his good. Horrid man that Semyon Ivanovitch! And what a nasty phiz he has!...'Flog him in the police station,' he said that on purpose. No, you are talking rubbish; you can flog, but I'm not going to; I shall punish Trifon with words, I shall punish him with reproaches, he will feel it. As for flogging, h'm!...it is an open question, h'm!...What about going to Emerance? Oh, damnation take it, the cursed pavement!" he cried out, suddenly tripping up. "And this is the capital. Enlightenment! One might break one's leg. H'm! I detest that Semyon Ivanovitch; a most revolting phiz. He was chuckling at me just now when I said they would embrace each other in a moral sense. Well, and they will embrace each other, and what's that to do with you? I am not going to embrace you; I'd rather embrace a peasant.... If I meet a peasant, I shall talk to him. I was drunk, though, and perhaps did not express myself properly. Possibly I am not expressing myself rightly now.... H'm! I shall never touch wine again. In the evening you babble, and next morning you are sorry for it. After all, I am walking quite steadily.... But they are all scoundrels, anyhow!"

So Ivan Ilyitch meditated incoherently and by snatches, as he went on striding along the pavement. The fresh air began to affect him, set his mind working. Five minutes later he would have felt soothed and sleepy. But all at once, scarcely two paces from the Great Prospect, he heard music. He looked round. On the other side of the street, in a very tumbledown-looking long wooden house of one storey, there was a great fête, there was the scraping of violins, and the droning of a double bass, and the squeaky tooting of a flute playing a very gay quadrille tune. Under the windows stood an audience, mainly of women in wadded pelisses with kerchiefs on their heads; they were straining every effort to see something through a crack in the shutters. Evidently there was a gay party within. The sound of the thud of dancing feet reached the other side of the street. Ivan Ilyitch saw a policeman standing not far off, and went up to him.

"Whose house is that, brother?" he asked, flinging his expensive fur coat open, just far enough to allow the policeman to see the imposing decoration on his breast.

"It belongs to the registration clerk Pseldonimov," answered the policeman, drawing himself up instantly, discerning the decoration.

"Pseldonimov? Bah! Pseldonimov! What is he up to? Getting married?"

"Yes, your Honour, to a daughter of a titular councillor, Mlekopitaev, a titular councillor... used to serve in the municipal department. That house goes with the bride."

"So that now the house is Pseldonimov's and not Mlekopitaev's?"

"Yes, Pseldonimov's, your Honour. It was Mlekopitaev's, but now it is Pseldonimov's."

"H'm! I am asking you, my man, because I am his chief. I am a general in the same office in which Pseldonimov serves."

"Just so, your Excellency."

The policeman drew himself up more stiffly than ever, while Ivan Ilyitch seemed to ponder. He stood still and meditated....

Yes, Pseldonimov really was in his department and in his own office; he remembered that. He was a little clerk with a salary of ten roubles a month. As Mr. Pralinsky had received his department very lately he might not have remembered precisely all his subordinates, but Pseldonimov he remembered just because of his surname. It had caught his eye from the very first, so that at the time he had had the curiosity to look with special attention at the possessor of such a surname. He remembered now a very young man with a long hooked nose, with tufts of flaxen hair, lean and ill-nourished, in an impossible uniform, and with unmentionables so impossible as to be actually unseemly; he remembered how the thought had flashed through his mind at the time: shouldn't he give the poor fellow ten roubles for Christmas, to spend on his wardrobe? But as the poor fellow's face was too austere, and his expression extremely unprepossessing, even exciting repulsion, the goodnatured idea somehow faded away of itself, so Pseldonimov did not get his tip. He had been the more surprised when this same Pseldonimov had not more than a week before asked for leave to be married. Ivan Ilyitch remembered that he had somehow not had time to go into the matter, so that the matter of the marriage had been settled offhand, in haste. But yet he did remember exactly that Pseldonimov was receiving a wooden house and four hundred roubles in cash as dowry with his bride. The circumstance had surprised him at the time; he remembered that he had made a slight jest over the juxtaposition of the names Pseldonimov and Mlekopitaev. He remembered all that clearly.

He recalled it, and grew more and more pensive. It is well known that whole trains of thought sometimes pass through our brains instantaneously as though they were sensations without being translated into human speech, still less into literary language. But we will try to translate these sensations of our hero's, and present to the reader at least the kernel of them, so to say, what was most essential and nearest to reality in them. For many of our sensations when translated into ordinary language seem absolutely unreal. That is why they never find expression, though every one has them. Of course Ivan Ilyitch's sensations and thoughts were a little incoherent. But you know the reason.

"Why," flashed through his mind, "here we all talk and talk, but when it comes to action — it all ends in nothing. Here, for instance, take this Pseldonimov: he has just come from his wedding full of hope and excitement, looking forward to his wedding feast.... This is one of the most blissful days of his life.... Now he is busy with his guests, is giving a banquet, a modest one, poor, but gay and full of genuine gladness.... What if he knew that at this very moment I, I, his superior, his chief, am standing by his house listening to the music? Yes, really how would he feel? No, what would he feel if I suddenly walked in? H'm!... Of course at first he would be frightened, he would be dumb with embarrassment.... I should be in his way, and perhaps should upset everything. Yes, that would be so if any other general went in, but not I.... That's a fact, any one else, but not I....

"Yes, Stepan Nikiforovitch! You did not understand me just now, but here is an example ready for you.

"Yes, we all make an outcry about acting humanely, but we are not capable of heroism, of fine actions.

"What sort of heroism? This sort. Consider: in the existing relations of the various members of society, for me, for me, after midnight to go in to the wedding of my subordinate, a registration clerk, at ten roubles the month — why, it would mean embarrassment, a revolution, the last days of Pompeii, a nonsensical folly. No one would understand it. Stepan Nikiforovitch would die before he understood it. Why, he said we should break down. Yes, but that's you old people, inert, paralytic people; but I shan't break down, I will transform the last day of Pompeii to a day of the utmost sweetness for my subordinate, and a wild action to an action normal, patriarchal, lofty and moral. How? Like this. Kindly listen....

"Here... I go in, suppose; they are amazed, leave off dancing, look wildly at me, draw back. Quite so, but at once I speak out: I go straight up to the frightened Pseldonimov, and with a most cordial, affable smile, in the simplest words, I say: 'This is how it is, I have been at his Excellency Stepan Nikiforovitch's. I expect you know, close here in the neighbourhood....'

Well, then, lightly, in a laughing way, I shall tell him of my adventure with Trifon. From Trifon I shall pass on to saying how I walked here on foot.... 'Well, I heard music, I inquired of a policeman, and learned, brother, that it was your wedding. Let me go in, I thought, to my subordinate's; let me see how my clerks enjoy themselves and...celebrate their wedding. I suppose you won't turn me out?' Turn me out! What a word for a subordinate! How the devil could he dream of turning me out! I fancy that he would be half crazy, that he would rush headlong to seat me in an armchair, would be trembling with delight, would hardly know what he was doing for the first minute!

"Why, what can be simpler, more elegant than such an action? Why did I go in? That's another question! That is, so to say, the moral aspect of the question. That's the pith.

"H'm, what was I thinking about, yes!

"Well, of course they will make me sit down with the most important guest, some titular councillor or a relation who's a retired captain with a red nose. Gogol describes these eccentrics so capitally. Well, I shall make acquaintance, of course, with the bride, I shall compliment her, I shall encourage the guests. I shall beg them not to stand on ceremony. To enjoy themselves, to go on dancing. I shall make jokes, I shall laugh; in fact, I shall be affable and charming. I am always affable and charming when I am pleased with myself.... H'm...the point is that I believe I am still a little, well, not drunk exactly, but...

"Of course, as a gentleman I shall be quite on an equality with them, and shall not expect any especial marks of.... But morally, morally, it is a different matter; they will understand and appreciate it.... My actions will evoke their nobler feelings.... Well, I shall stay for half an hour... even for an hour; I shall leave, of course, before supper; but they will be bustling about, baking and roasting, they will be making low bows, but I will only drink a glass, congratulate them and refuse supper. I shall say —'business.' And as soon as I pronounce the word 'business,' all of them will at once have sternly respectful faces. By that I shall delicately remind them that there is a difference between them and me. The earth and the sky. It is not that I want to impress that on them, but it must be done...it's even essential in a moral sense, when all is said and done. I shall smile at once, however, I shall even laugh, and then they will all pluck up courage again.... I shall jest a little again with the bride; h'm!...I may even hint that I shall come again in just nine months to stand godfather, he-he! And she will be sure to be brought to bed by then. They multiply, you know, like rabbits. And they will all roar with laughter and the bride will blush; I shall kiss her feelingly on the forehead, even give her my blessing...and next day my exploit will be known at the office. Next day I shall be stern again, next day I shall be exacting again, even implacable, but they will all know what I am like. They will know my heart, they will know my essential nature: 'He is stern as chief, but as a man he is an angel!' And I shall have conquered them; I shall have captured them by one little act which would never have entered your head; they would be mine; I should be their father, they would be my children.... Come now, your Excellency Stepan Nikiforovitch, go and do likewise....

"But do you know, do you understand, that Pseldonimov will tell his children how the General himself feasted and even drank at his wedding! Why you know those children would tell their children, and those would tell their grandchildren as a most sacred story that a grand gentleman, a statesman (and I shall be all that by then) did them the honour, and so on, and so on. Why, I am morally elevating the humiliated, I restore him to himself.... Why, he gets a salary of ten roubles a month!...If I repeat this five or ten times, or something of the sort, I shall gain popularity all over the place.... My name will be printed on the hearts of all, and the devil only knows what will come of that popularity!..."

These, or something like these, were Ivan Ilyitch's reflections, (a man says all sorts of things sometimes to himself, gentlemen, especially when he is in rather an eccentric condition). All these meditations passed through his mind in something like half a minute, and of course he might have confined himself to these dreams and, after mentally putting Stepan Nikiforovitch to shame, have gone very peacefully home and to bed. And he would have done well. But the trouble of it was that the moment was an eccentric one.

As ill-luck would have it, at that very instant the selfsatisfied faces of Stepan Nikiforovitch and Semyon Ivanovitch suddenly rose before his heated imagination.

"We shall break down!" repeated Stepan Nikiforovitch, smiling disdainfully.

"He-he-he," Semyon Ivanovitch seconded him with his nastiest smile.

"Well, we'll see whether we do break down!" Ivan Ilyitch said resolutely, with a rush of heat to his face.

He stepped down from the pavement and with resolute steps went straight across the street towards the house of his registration clerk Pseldonimov.

His star carried him away. He walked confidently in at the open gate and contemptuously thrust aside with his foot the shaggy, husky little sheep-dog who flew at his legs with a hoarse bark, more as a matter of form than with any real intention. Along a wooden plank he went to the covered porch which led like a sentry box to the yard, and by three decaying wooden steps he went up to the tiny entry. Here, though a tallow candle or something in the way of a nightlight was burning somewhere in a corner, it did not prevent Ivan Ilyitch from putting his left foot just as it was, in its galosh, into a galantine which had been stood out there to cool. Ivan Ilyitch bent down, and looking with curiosity, he saw that there were two other dishes of some sort of jelly and also two shapes apparently of blancmange. The squashed galantine embarrassed him, and for one brief instant the thought flashed through his mind, whether he should not slink away at once. But he considered this too low. Reflecting that no one would have seen him, and that they would never think he had done it, he hurriedly wiped his galosh to conceal all traces, fumbled for the felt-covered door, opened it and found himself in a very little anteroom. Half of it was literally piled up with greatcoats, wadded jackets, cloaks, capes, scarves and galoshes. In the other half the musicians had been installed; two violins, a flute, and a double bass, a band of four, picked up, of course, in the street. They were sitting at an unpainted wooden table, lighted by a single tallow candle, and with the utmost vigour were sawing out the last figure of the quadrille. From the open door into the drawing-room one could see the dancers in the midst of dust, tobacco smoke and fumes. There was a frenzy of gaiety. There were sounds of laughter, shouts and shrieks from the ladies. The gentlemen stamped like a squadron of horses. Above all the Bedlam there rang out words of command from the leader of the dance, probably an extremely free and easy, and even unbuttoned gentleman: "Gentlemen advance, ladies' chain, set to partners!" and so on, and so on. Ivan Ilyitch in some excitement cast off his coat and galoshes, and with his cap in his hand went into the room. He was no longer reflecting, however.

For the first minute nobody noticed him; all were absorbed in dancing the quadrille to the end. Ivan Ilyitch stood as though entranced, and could make out nothing definite in the chaos. He caught glimpses of ladies' dresses, of gentlemen with cigarettes between their teeth. He caught a glimpse of a lady's pale blue scarf which flicked him on the nose. After the wearer a medical student, with his hair blown in all directions on his head, pranced by in wild delight and jostled violently against him on the way. He caught a glimpse, too, of an officer of some description, who looked half a mile high. Some one in an unnaturally shrill voice shouted, "O-o-oh, Pseldonimov!" as the speaker flew by stamping. It was sticky under Ivan Ilyitch's feet; evidently the floor had been waxed. In the room, which was a very small one, there were about thirty people.

But a minute later the quadrille was over, and almost at once the very thing Ivan Ilyitch had pictured when he was dreaming on the pavement took place.

A stifled murmur, a strange whisper passed over the whole company, including the dancers, who had not yet had time to take breath and wipe their perspiring faces. All eyes, all faces began quickly turning towards the newly arrived guest. Then they all seemed to draw back a little and beat a retreat. Those who had not noticed him were pulled by their coats or dresses and informed. They looked round and at once beat a retreat with the others. Ivan Ilyitch was still standing at the door without moving a step forward, and between him and the company there stretched an ever widening empty space of floor strewn with countless sweetmeat wrappings, bits of paper and cigarette ends. All at once a young man in a uniform, with a shock of flaxen hair and a hooked nose, stepped timidly out into that empty space. He moved forward, hunched up, and looked at the unexpected visitor exactly with the expression with which a dog looks at its master when the latter has called him up and is going to kick him.

"Good evening, Pseldonimov, do you know me?" said Ivan Ilyitch, and felt at the same minute that he had said this very awkwardly; he felt, too, that he was perhaps doing something horribly stupid at that moment.

"You-our Ex-cel-len-cy!" muttered Pseldonimov.

"To be sure.... I have called in to see you quite by chance, my friend, as you can probably imagine...."

But evidently Pseldonimov could imagine nothing. He stood with staring eyes in the utmost perplexity.

"You won't turn me out, I suppose.... Pleased or not, you must make a visitor welcome...." Ivan Ilyitch went on, feeling that he was confused to a point of unseemly feebleness; that he was trying to smile and was utterly unable; that the humorous reference to Stepan Nikiforovitch and Trifon was becoming more and more impossible. But as ill luck would have it, Pseldonimov did not recover from his stupefaction, and still gazed at him with a perfectly idiotic air. Ivan Ilyitch winced, he felt that in another minute something incredibly foolish would happen.

"I am not in the way, am I?... I'll go away," he faintly articulated, and there was a tremor at the right corner of his mouth.

But Pseldonimov had recovered himself.

"Good heavens, your Excellency... the honour...," he muttered, bowing hurriedly. "Graciously sit down, your Excellency...." And recovering himself still further, he motioned him with both hands to a sofa before which a table had been moved away to make room for the dancing.

Ivan Ilyitch felt relieved and sank on the sofa; at once some one flew to move the table up to him. He took a cursory look round and saw that he was the only person sitting down, all the others were standing, even the ladies. A bad sign. But it was not yet time to reassure and encourage them. The company still held back, while before him, bending double, stood Pseldonimov, utterly alone, still completely at a loss and very far from smiling. It was horrid; in short, our hero endured such misery at that moment that his Haroun al-Raschid-like descent upon his subordinates for the sake of principle might well have been reckoned an heroic action. But suddenly a little figure made its appearance beside Pseldonimov, and began bowing. To his inexpressible pleasure and even happiness, Ivan Ilyitch at once recognised him as the head clerk of his office, Akim Petrovitch Zubikov, and though, of course, he was not acquainted with him, he knew him to be a businesslike and exemplary clerk. He got up at once and held out his hand to Akim Petrovitch — his whole hand, not two fingers. The latter took it in both of his with the deepest respect. The general was triumphant, the situation was saved.

And now indeed Pseldonimov was no longer, so to say, the second person, but the third. It was possible to address his remarks to the head clerk in his necessity, taking him for an acquaintance and even an intimate one, and Pseldonimov meanwhile could only be silent and be in a tremor of reverence. So that the proprieties were observed. And some explanation was essential, Ivan Ilyitch felt that; he saw that all the guests were expecting something, that the whole household was gathered together in the doorway, almost creeping, climbing over one another in their anxiety to see and hear him. What was horrid was that the head clerk in his foolishness remained standing.

"Why are you standing?" said Ivan Ilyitch, awkwardly motioning him to a seat on the sofa beside him.

"Oh, don't trouble.... I'll sit here." And Akim Petrovitch hurriedly sat down on a chair, almost as it was being put for him by Pseldonimov, who remained obstinately standing.

"Can you imagine what happened," addressing himself exclusively to Akim Petrovitch in a rather quavering, though free and easy voice. He even drawled out his words, with special emphasis on some syllables, pronounced the vowel *ah* like *eh*; in short, felt and was conscious that he was being affected but could not control himself: some external force was at work. He was painfully conscious of many things at that moment.

"Can you imagine, I have only just come from Stepan Nikiforovitch Nikiforov's, you have heard of him perhaps, the privy councillor. You know...on that special committee...."

Akim Petrovitch bent his whole person forward respectfully: as much as to say, "Of course we have heard of him."

"He is your neighbor now," Ivan Ilyitch went on, for one instant for the sake of ease and good manners addressing Pseldonimov, but he quickly turned away again, on seeing from the latter's eyes that it made absolutely no difference to him.

"The old fellow, as you know, has been dreaming all his life of buying himself a house.... Well, and he has bought it. And a very pretty house too. Yes.... And to-day was his birthday and he had never celebrated it before, he used even to keep it secret from us, he was too stingy to keep it, he-he. But now he is so delighted over his new house, that he invited Semyon Ivanovitch Shipulenko and me, you know."

Akim Petrovitch bent forward again. He bent forward zealously. Ivan Ilyitch felt somewhat comforted. It had struck him, indeed, that the head clerk possibly was guessing that he was an indispensable *point d'appui* for his Excellency at that moment. That would have been more horrid than anything.

"So we sat together, the three of us, he gave us champagne, we talked about problems... even dis-pu-ted.... He-he!"

Akim Petrovitch raised his eyebrows respectfully.

"Only that is not the point. When I take leave of him at last — he is a punctual old fellow, goes to bed early, you know, in his old age —I go out.... My Trifon is nowhere to be seen! I am anxious, I make inquiries. 'What has Trifon done with the carriage?' It comes out that hoping I should stay on, he had gone off to the wedding of some friend of his, or sister maybe.... Goodness only knows. Somewhere here on the Petersburg Side. And took the carriage with him while he was about it."

Again for the sake of good manners the general glanced in the direction of Pseldonimov. The latter promptly gave a wriggle, but not at all the sort of wriggle the general would have liked. "He has no sympathy, no heart," flashed through his brain.

"You don't say so!" said Akim Petrovitch, greatly impressed. A faint murmur of surprise ran through all the crowd.

"Can you fancy my position...." (Ivan Ilyitch glanced at them all.) "There was nothing for it, I set off on foot, I thought I would trudge to the Great Prospect, and there find some cabby...he-he!"

"He-he-he!" Akim Petrovitch echoed. Again a murmur, but this time on a more cheerful note, passed through the crowd. At that moment the chimney of a lamp on the wall broke with a crash. Some one rushed zealously to see to it. Pseldonimov started and looked sternly at the lamp, but the general took no notice of it, and all was serene again.

"I walked...and the night was so lovely, so still. All at once I heard a band, stamping, dancing. I inquired of a policeman; it is Pseldonimov's wedding. Why, you are giving a ball to all Petersburg Side, my friend. Ha-ha." He turned to Pseldonimov again.

"He-he-he! To be sure," Akim Petrovitch responded. There was a stir among the guests again, but what was most foolish was that Pseldonimov, though he bowed, did not even now smile, but seemed as though he were made of wood. "Is he a fool or what?" thought Ivan Ilyitch. "He ought to have smiled at that point, the ass, and everything would have run easily." There was a fury of impatience in his heart.

"I thought I would go in to see my clerk. He won't turn me out I expect...pleased or not, one must welcome a guest. You must please excuse me, my dear fellow. If I am in the way, I will go...I only came in to have a look...."

But little by little a general stir was beginning.

Akim Petrovitch looked at him with a mawkishly sweet expression as though to say, "How could your Excellency be in the way?" all the guests stirred and began to display the first symptoms of being at their ease. Almost all the ladies sat down. A good sign and a reassuring one. The boldest spirits among them fanned themselves with their handkerchiefs. One of them in a shabby velvet dress said something with intentional loudness. The officer addressed by her would have liked to answer her as loudly, but seeing that they were the only ones speaking aloud, he subsided. The men, for the most part government clerks, with two or three students among them, looked at one another as though egging each other on to unbend, cleared their throats, and began to move a few steps in different directions. No one, however, was particularly timid, but they were all restive, and almost all of them looked with a hostile expression at the personage who had burst in upon them, to destroy their gaiety. The officer, ashamed of his cowardice, began to edge up to the table.

"But I say, my friend, allow me to ask you your name," Ivan Ilyitch asked Pseldonimov.

"Porfiry Petrovitch, your Excellency," answered the latter, with staring eyes as though on parade.

"Introduce me, Porfiry Petrovitch, to your bride.... Take me to her...I...."

And he showed signs of a desire to get up. But Pseldonimov ran full speed to the drawing-room. The bride, however, was standing close by at the door, but as soon as she heard herself mentioned, she hid. A minute later Pseldonimov led her up by the hand. The guests all moved aside to make way for them. Ivan Ilyitch got up solemnly and addressed himself to her with a most affable smile.

"Very, very much pleased to make your acquaintance," he pronounced with a most aristocratic half-bow, "especially on such a day...."

He gave a meaning smile. There was an agreeable flutter among the ladies.

"*Charmé*," the lady in the velvet dress pronounced, almost aloud.

The bride was a match for Pseldonimov. She was a thin little lady not more than seventeen, pale, with a very small face and a sharp little nose. Her quick, active little eyes were not at all embarrassed; on the contrary, they looked at him steadily and even with a shade of resentment. Evidently Pseldonimov was marrying her for her beauty. She was dressed in a white muslin dress over a pink slip. Her neck was thin, and she had a figure like a chicken's with the bones all sticking out. She was not equal to making any response to the general's affability.

"But she is very pretty," he went on, in an undertone, as though addressing Pseldonimov only, though intentionally speaking so that the bride could hear.

But on this occasion, too, Pseldonimov again answered absolutely nothing, and did not even wriggle. Ivan Ilyitch fancied that there was something cold, suppressed in his eyes, as though he had something peculiarly malignant in his mind. And yet he had at all costs to wring some sensibility out of him. Why, that was the object of his coming.

"They are a couple, though!" he thought.

And he turned again to the bride, who had seated herself beside him on the sofa, but in answer to his two or three questions he got nothing but "yes" or "no," and hardly that.

"If only she had been overcome with confusion," he thought to himself, "then I should have begun to banter her. But as it is, my position is impossible."

And as ill-luck would have it, Akim Petrovitch, too, was mute; though this was only due to his foolishness, it was still unpardonable.

"My friends! Haven't I perhaps interfered with your enjoyment?" he said, addressing the whole company.

He felt that the very palms of his hands were perspiring.

"No...don't trouble, your Excellency; we are beginning directly, but now...we are getting cool," answered the officer.

The bride looked at him with pleasure; the officer was not old, and wore the uniform of some branch of the service. Pseldonimov was still standing in the same place, bending forward, and it seemed as though his hooked nose stood out further than ever. He looked and listened like a footman standing with the greatcoat on his arm, waiting for the end of his master's farewell conversation. Ivan Ilyitch made this comparison himself. He was losing his head; he felt that he was in an awkward position, that the ground was giving way under his feet, that he had got in somewhere and could not find his way out, as though he were in the dark.

Suddenly the guests all moved aside, and a short, thickset, middle-aged woman made her appearance, dressed plainly though she was in her best, with a big shawl on her shoulders, pinned at her throat, and on her head a cap to which she was evidently unaccustomed. In her hands she carried a small round tray on which stood a full but uncorked bottle of champagne and two glasses, neither more nor less. Evidently the bottle was intended for only two guests.

The middle-aged lady approached the general.

"Don't look down on us, your Excellency," she said, bowing. "Since you have deigned to do my son the honour of coming to his wedding, we beg you graciously to drink to the health of the young people. Do not disdain us; do us the honour."

Ivan Ilyitch clutched at her as though she were his salvation. She was by no means an old woman — forty-five or forty-six, not more; but she had such a goodnatured, rosy-cheeked, such a round and candid Russian face, she smiled so goodhumouredly, bowed so simply, that Ivan Ilyitch was almost comforted and began to hope again.

"So you are the moother of your so-on?" he said, getting up from the sofa.

"Yes, my mother, your Excellency," mumbled Pseldonimov, craning his long neck and thrusting forward his long nose again.

"Ah! I am delighted — de-ligh-ted to make your acquaintance."

"Do not refuse us, your Excellency."

"With the greatest pleasure."

The tray was put down. Pseldonimov dashed forward to pour out the wine. Ivan Ilyitch, still standing, took the glass.

"I am particularly, particularly glad on this occasion, that I can ..," he began, "that I can... testify before all of you.... In short, as your chief... I wish you, madam" (he turned to the bride), "and you, friend Porfiry, I wish you the fullest, completest happiness for many long years."

And he positively drained the glass with feeling, the seventh he had drunk that evening. Pseldonimov looked at him gravely and even sullenly. The general was beginning to feel an agonising hatred of him.

"And that scarecrow" (he looked at the officer) "keeps obtruding himself. He might at least have shouted 'hurrah!' and it would have gone off, it would have gone off...."

"And you too, Akim Petrovitch, drink a glass to their health," added the mother, addressing the head clerk. "You are his superior, he is under you. Look after my boy, I beg you as a mother. And don't forget us in the future, our good, kind friend, Akim Petrovitch."

"How nice these old Russian women are," thought Ivan Ilyitch. "She has livened us all up. I have always loved the democracy...."

At that moment another tray was brought to the table; it was brought in by a maid wearing a crackling cotton dress that had never been washed, and a crinoline. She could hardly grasp the tray in both hands, it was so big. On it there were numbers of plates of apples, sweets, fruit meringues and fruit cheeses, walnuts and so on, and so on. The tray had been till then in the drawing-room for the delectation of all the guests, and especially the ladies. But now it was brought to the general alone.

"Do not disdain our humble fare, your Excellency. What we have we are pleased to offer," the old lady repeated, bowing.

"Delighted!" said Ivan Ilyitch, and with real pleasure took a walnut and cracked it between his fingers. He had made up his mind to win popularity at all costs.

Meantime the bride suddenly giggled.

"What is it?" asked Ivan Ilyitch with a smile, encouraged by this sign of life.

"Ivan Kostenkinitch, here, makes me laugh," she answered, looking down.

The general distinguished, indeed, a flaxen-headed young man, exceedingly good-looking, who was sitting on a chair at the other end of the sofa, whispering something to Madame Pseldonimov. The young man stood up. He was apparently very young and very shy.

"I was telling the lady about a 'dream book,' your Excellency," he muttered as though apologising.

"About what sort of 'dream book'?" asked Ivan Ilyitch condescendingly.

"There is a new 'dream book,' a literary one. I was telling the lady that to dream of Mr. Panaev means spilling coffee on one's shirt front."

"What innocence!" thought Ivan Ilyitch, with positive annoyance.

Though the young man flushed very red as he said it, he was incredibly delighted that he had said this about Mr. Panaev.

"To be sure, I have heard of it...," responded his Excellency.

"No, there is something better than that," said a voice quite close to Ivan Ilyitch. "There is a new encyclopædia being published, and they say Mr. Kraevsky will write articles...and satirical literature."

This was said by a young man who was by no means embarrassed, but rather free and easy. He was wearing gloves and a white waistcoat, and carried a hat in his hand. He did not dance, and looked condescending, for he was on the staff of a satirical paper called *The Firebrand*, and gave himself airs accordingly. He had come casually to the wedding, invited as an honoured guest of the Pseldonimovs', with whom he was on intimate terms and with whom only a year before he had lived in very poor lodgings, kept by a German woman. He drank vodka, however, and for that purpose had more than once withdrawn to a snug little back room to which all the guests knew their way. The general disliked him extremely.

"And the reason that's funny," broke in joyfully the flaxen-headed young man, who had talked of the shirt front and at whom the young man on the comic paper looked with hatred in consequence, "it's funny, your Excellency, because it is supposed by the writer that Mr. Kraevsky does not know how to spell, and thinks that 'satirical' ought to be written with a 'y' instead of an 'i.'"

But the poor young man scarcely finished his sentence; he could see from his eyes that the general knew all this long ago, for the general himself looked embarrassed, and evidently because he knew it. The young man seemed inconceivably ashamed. He succeeded in effacing himself completely, and remained very melancholy all the rest of the evening.

But to make up for that the young man on the staff of the *Firebrand* came up nearer, and seemed to be intending to sit down somewhere close by. Such free and easy manners struck Ivan Ilyitch as rather shocking.

"Tell me, please, Porfiry," he began, in order to say something, "why — I have always wanted to ask you about it in person — why you are called Pseldonimov instead of Pseudonimov? Your name surely must be Pseudonimov."

"I cannot inform you exactly, your Excellency," said Pseldonimov.

"It must have been that when his father went into the service they made a mistake in his papers, so that he has remained now Pseldonimov," put in Akim Petrovitch. "That does happen."

"Undoubted-ly," the general said with warmth, "undoubted-ly; for only think, Pseudonimov comes from the literary word pseudonym, while Pseldonimov means nothing."

"Due to foolishness," added Akim Petrovitch.

"You mean what is due to foolishness?"

"The Russian common people in their foolishness often alter letters, and sometimes pronounce them in their own way. For instance, they say nevalid instead of invalid."

"Oh, yes, nevalid, he-he-he...."

"Mumber, too, they say, your Excellency," boomed out the tall officer, who had long been itching to distinguish himself in some way.

"What do you mean by mumber?"

"Mumber instead of number, your Excellency."

"Oh, yes, mumber...instead of number.... To be sure, to be sure.... He-he-he!" Ivan Ilyitch had to do a chuckle for the benefit of the officer too.

The officer straightened his tie.

"Another thing they say is nigh by," the young man on the comic paper put in. But his Excellency tried not to hear this. His chuckles were not at everybody's disposal.

"Nigh by, instead of near," the young man on the comic paper persisted, in evident irritation. Ivan Ilyitch looked at him sternly.

"Come, why persist?" Pseldonimov whispered to him.

"Why, I was talking. Mayn't one speak?" the latter protested in a whisper; but he said no more and with secret fury walked out of the room.

He made his way straight to the attractive little back room where, for the benefit of the dancing gentlemen, vodka of two sorts, salt fish, caviare into slices and a bottle of very strong sherry of Russian make had been set early in the evening on a little table, covered with a Yaroslav cloth. With anger in his heart he was pouring himself out a glass of vodka, when suddenly the medical student with the dishevelled locks, the foremost dancer and cutter of capers at Pseldonimov's ball, rushed in. He fell on the decanter with greedy haste.

"They are just going to begin!" he said rapidly, helping himself. "Come and look, I am going to dance a solo on my head; after supper I shall risk the fish dance. It is just the thing for the wedding. So to speak, a friendly hint to Pseldonimov. She's a jolly creature that Kleopatra Semyonovna, you can venture on anything you like with her."

"He's a reactionary," said the young man on the comic paper gloomily, as he tossed off his vodka.

"Who is a reactionary?"

"Why, the personage before whom they set those sweetmeats. He's a reactionary, I tell you."

"What nonsense!" muttered the student, and he rushed out of the room, hearing the opening bars of the quadrille.

Left alone, the young man on the comic paper poured himself out another glass to give himself more assurance and independence; he drank and ate a snack of something, and never had the actual civil councillor Ivan Ilyitch made for himself a bitterer foe more implacably bent on revenge than was the young man on the staff of the *Firebrand* whom he had so slighted, especially after the latter had drunk two glasses of vodka. Alas! Ivan Ilyitch suspected nothing of the sort. He did not suspect another circumstance of prime importance either, which had an influence on the mutual relations of the guests and his Excellency. The fact was that though he had given a proper and even detailed explanation of his presence at his clerk's wedding, this explanation did not really satisfy any one, and the visitors were still embarrassed. But suddenly everything was transformed as though by magic, all were reassured and ready to enjoy themselves, to laugh, to shriek; to dance, exactly as though the unexpected visitor were not in the room. The cause of it was a rumour, a whisper, a report which spread in some unknown way that the visitor was not quite...it seemed — was, in fact, "a little top-heavy." And though this seemed at first a horrible calumny, it began by degrees to appear to be justified; suddenly everything became clear. What was more, they felt all at once extraordinarily free. And it was just at this moment that the quadrille for which the medical student was in such haste, the last before supper, began.

And just as Ivan Ilyitch meant to address the bride again, intending to provoke her with some innuendo, the tall officer suddenly dashed up to her and with a flourish dropped on one knee before her. She immediately jumped up from the sofa, and whisked off with him to take her place in the quadrille. The officer did not even apologise, and she did not even glance at the general as she went away; she seemed, in fact, relieved to escape.

"After all she has a right to be,' thought Ivan Ilyitch, 'and of course they don't know how to behave.' "Hm! Don't you stand on ceremony, friend Porfiry," he said, addressing Pseldonimov. "Perhaps you have...arrangements to make...or something...please don't put yourself out.' 'Why does he keep guard over me?'" he thought to himself.

Pseldonimov, with his long neck and his eyes fixed intently upon him, began to be insufferable. In fact, all this was not the thing, not the thing at all, but Ivan Ilyitch was still far from admitting this.

The quadrille began.

"Will you allow me, your Excellency?" asked Akim Petrovitch, holding the bottle respectfully in his hands and preparing to pour from it into his Excellency's glass.

"I... I really don't know, whether...."

But Akim Petrovitch, with reverent and radiant face, was already filling the glass. After filling the glass, he proceeded, writhing and wriggling, as it were stealthily, as it were furtively, to pour himself out some, with this difference, that he did not fill his own glass to within a finger length of the top, and this seemed somehow more respectful. He was like a woman in travail as he sat beside his chief. What could he talk about, indeed? Yet to entertain his Excellency was an absolute duty since he had the honour of keeping him company. The champagne served as a resource, and his Excellency, too, was pleased that he had filled his glass — not for the sake of the champagne, for it was warm and perfectly abominable, but just morally pleased.

"The old chap would like to have a drink himself," thought Ivan Ilyitch, "but he doesn't venture till I do. I mustn't prevent him. And indeed it would be absurd for the bottle to stand between as untouched."

He took a sip, anyway it seemed better than sitting doing nothing.

"I am here," he said, with pauses and emphasis, "I am here, you know, so to speak, accidentally, and, of course, it may be... that some people would consider... it unseemly for me to be at such... a gathering."

Akim Petrovitch said nothing, but listened with timid curiosity.

"But I hope you will understand, with what object I have come.... I haven't really come simply to drink wine... he-he!"

Akim Petrovitch tried to chuckle, following the example of his Excellency, but again he could not get it out, and again he made absolutely no consolatory answer.

"I am here... in order, so to speak, to encourage... to show, so to speak, a moral aim," Ivan Ilyitch continued, feeling vexed at Akim Petrovitch's stupidity, but he suddenly subsided into silence himself. He saw that poor Akim Petrovitch had dropped his eyes as though he were in fault. The general in some confusion made haste to take another sip from his glass, and Akim Petrovitch clutched at the bottle as though it were his only hope of salvation and filled the glass again.

"You haven't many resources," thought Ivan Ilyitch, looking sternly at poor Akim Petrovitch. The latter, feeling that stern general-like eye upon him, made up his mind to remain silent for good and not to raise his eyes. So they sat beside each other for a couple of minutes — two sickly minutes for Akim Petrovitch.

A couple of words about Akim Petrovitch. He was a man of the old school, as meek as a hen, reared from infancy to obsequious servility, and at the same time a goodnatured and even honourable man. He was a Petersburg Russian; that is, his father and his father's father were born, grew up and served in Petersburg and had never once left Petersburg. That is quite a special type of Russian. They have hardly any idea of Russia, though that does not trouble them at all. Their whole interest is confined to Petersburg and chiefly the place in which they serve. All their thoughts are concentrated on preference for farthing points, on the shop, and their month's salary. They don't know a single Russian custom, a single Russian song except "Lutchinushka," and that only because it is played on the barrel organs. However, there are two fundamental and invariable signs by which you can at once distinguish a Petersburg Russian from a real Russian. The first sign is the fact that Petersburg Russians, all without exception, speak of the newspaper as the *Academic News* and never call it the *Petersburg News*. The second and equally trustworthy sign is that Petersburg Russians never make use of the word "breakfast," but always call it "Frühstück" with especial emphasis on the first syllable. By these radical and distinguishing signs you can tell them apart; in short, this is a humble type which has been formed during the last thirty-five years. Akim Petrovitch, however, was by no means a fool. If the general had asked him a question about anything in his own province he would have answered and kept up a conversation; as it was, it was unseemly for a subordinate even to answer such questions as these, though Akim Petrovitch was dying from curiosity to know something more detailed about his Excellency's real intentions.

And meanwhile Ivan Ilyitch sank more and more into meditation and a sort of whirl of ideas; in his absorption he sipped his glass every half-minute. Akim Petrovitch at once zealously filled it up. Both were silent. Ivan Ilyitch began looking at the dances, and immediately something attracted his attention. One circumstance even surprised him....

The dances were certainly lively. Here people danced in the simplicity of their hearts to amuse themselves and even to romp wildly. Among the dancers few were really skilful, but the unskilled stamped so vigorously that they might have been taken for agile ones. The officer was among the foremost; he particularly liked the figures in which he was left alone, to perform a solo. Then he performed the most marvellous capers. For instance, standing upright as a post, he would suddenly bend over to one side, so that one expected him to fall over; but with the next step he would suddenly bend over in the opposite direction at the same acute angle to the floor. He kept the most serious face and danced in the full conviction that every one was watching him. Another gentleman, who had had rather more than he could carry before the quadrille, dropped asleep beside his partner so that his partner had to dance alone. The young registration clerk, who had danced with the lady in the blue scarf through all the figures and through all the five quadrilles which they had danced that evening, played the same prank the whole time: that is, he dropped a little behind his partner, seized the end of her scarf, and as they crossed over succeeded in imprinting some twenty kisses on the scarf. His partner sailed along in front of him, as though she noticed nothing. The medical student really did dance on his head, and excited frantic enthusiasm, stamping, and shrieks of delight. In short, the absence of constraint was very marked. Ivan Ilyitch, whom the wine was beginning to affect, began by smiling, but by degrees a bitter doubt began to steal into his heart; of course he liked free and easy manners and unconventionality. He desired, he had even inwardly prayed for free and easy manners, when they had all held back, but now that unconventionality had gone beyond all limits. One lady, for instance, the one in the shabby dark blue velvet dress, bought fourth-hand, in the sixth figure pinned her dress so as to turn it into — something like trousers. This was the Kleopatra Semyonovna with whom one could venture to do anything, as her partner, the medical student, had expressed it. The medical student defied description: he was simply a Fokin. How was it? They had held back and now they were so quickly emancipated! One might think it nothing, but this transformation was somehow strange; it indicated something. It was as though they had forgotten Ivan Ilyitch's existence. Of course he was the first to laugh, and even ventured to applaud. Akim Petrovitch chuckled respectfully in unison, though, indeed, with evident pleasure and no suspicion that his Excellency was beginning to nourish in his heart a new gnawing anxiety.

"You dance capitally, young man," Ivan Ilyitch was obliged to say to the medical student as he walked past him.

The student turned sharply towards him, made a grimace, and bringing his face close into unseemly proximity to the face of his Excellency, crowed like a cock at the top of his voice. This was too much. Ivan Ilyitch got up from the table. In spite of that, a roar of inexpressible laughter followed, for the crow was an extraordinarily good imitation, and the whole performance was utterly unexpected. Ivan Ilyitch was still standing in bewilderment, when suddenly Pseldonimov himself made his appearance, and with a bow, began begging him to come to supper. His mother followed him.

"Your Excellency," she said, bowing, "do us the honour, do not disdain our humble fare."

"I...I really don't know," Ivan Ilyitch was beginning. "I did not come with that idea...I... meant to be going...."

He was, in fact, holding his hat in his hands. What is more, he had at that very moment taken an inward vow at all costs to depart at once and on no account whatever to consent to remain, and...he remained. A minute later he led the procession to the table. Pseldonimov and his mother walked in front, clearing the way for him. They made him sit down in the seat of honour, and again a bottle of champagne, opened but not begun, was set beside his plate. By way of *hors d'œuvres* there were salt herrings and vodka. He put out his hand, poured out a large glass of vodka and drank it off. He had never drunk vodka before. He felt as though he were rolling down a hill, were flying, flying, flying, that he must stop himself, catch at something, but there was no possibility of it.

His position was certainly becoming more and more eccentric. What is more, it seemed as though fate were mocking at him. God knows what had happened to him in the course of an hour or so. When he went in he had, so to say, opened his arms to embrace all humanity, all his subordinates; and here not more than an hour had passed and in all his aching heart he felt and knew that he hated Pseldonimov and was cursing him, his wife and his wedding. What was more, he saw from his face, from his eyes alone, that Pseldonimov himself hated him, that he was looking at him with eyes that almost said: "If only you would take yourself off, curse you! Foisting yourself on us!" All this he had read for some time in his eyes.

Of course as he sat down to table, Ivan Ilyitch would sooner have had his hand cut off than have owned, not only aloud, but even to himself, that this was really so. The moment had not fully arrived yet. There was still a moral vacillation. But his heart, his heart...it ached! It was clamouring for freedom, for air, for rest. Ivan Ilyitch was really too goodnatured.

He knew, of course, that he ought long before to have gone away, not merely to have gone away but to have made his escape. That all this was not the same, but had turned out utterly different from what he had dreamed of on the pavement.

"Why did I come? Did I come here to eat and drink?" he asked himself as he tasted the salt herring. He even had attacks of scepticism. There was at moments a faint stir of irony in regard to his own fine action at the bottom of his heart. He actually wondered at times why he had come in.

But how could he go away? To go away like this without having finished the business properly was impossible. What would people say? They would say that he was frequenting low company. Indeed it really would amount to that if he did not end it properly. What would Stepan Nikiforovitch, Semyon Ivanovitch say (for of course it would be all over the place by tomorrow)? what would be said in the offices, at the Shembels', at the Shubins'? No, he must take his departure in such a way that all should understand why he had come, he must make clear his moral aim.... And meantime the dramatic moment would not present itself. "They don't even respect me," he went on, thinking. "What are they laughing at? They are as free and easy as though they had no feeling.... But I have long suspected that all the younger generation are without feeling! I must remain at all costs! They have just been dancing, but now at table they will all be gathered together.... I will talk about questions, about reforms, about the greatness of Russia.... I can still win their enthusiasm! Yes! Perhaps nothing is yet lost.... Perhaps it is always like this in reality. What should I begin upon with them to attract them? What plan can I hit upon? I am lost, simply lost.... And what is it they want, what is it they require?...I see they are laughing together there. Can it be at me, merciful heavens! But what is it I want... why is it I am here, why don't I go away, why do I go on persisting?"...He thought this, and a sort of shame, a deep unbearable shame, rent his heart more and more intensely.

But everything went on in the same way, one thing after another.

Just two minutes after he had sat down to the table one terrible thought overwhelmed him completely. He suddenly felt that he was horribly drunk, that is, not as he was before, but hopelessly drunk. The cause of this was the glass of vodka which he had drunk after the champagne, and which had immediately produced an effect. He was conscious, he felt in every fibre of his being that he was growing hopelessly feeble. Of course his assurance was greatly increased, but consciousness had not deserted him, and it kept crying out: "It is bad, very bad and, in fact, utterly unseemly!" Of course his unstable drunken reflections could not rest long on one subject; there began to be apparent and unmistakably so, even to himself, two opposite sides. On one side there was swaggering assurance, a desire to conquer, a disdain of obstacles and a desperate confidence that he would attain his object. The other side showed itself in the aching of his heart, and a sort of gnawing in his soul. "What would they say? How would it all end? What would happen tomorrow, tomorrow, tomorrow?"...

He had felt vaguely before that he had enemies in the company. "No doubt that was because I was drunk," he thought with agonising doubt. What was his horror when he actually, by unmistakable signs, convinced himself now that he really had enemies at the table, and that it was impossible to doubt of it.

"And why — why?" he wondered.

At the table there were all the thirty guests, of whom several were quite tipsy. Others were behaving with a careless and sinister independence, shouting and talking at the top of their voices, bawling out the toasts before the time, and pelting the ladies with pellets of bread. One unprepossessing personage in a greasy coat had fallen off his chair as soon as he sat down, and remained so till the end of supper. Another one made desperate efforts to stand on the table, to propose a toast, and only the officer, who seized him by the tails of his coat, moderated his premature ardour. The supper was a pell-mell affair, although they had hired a cook who had been in the service of a general; there was the galantine, there was tongue and potatoes, there were rissoles with green peas, there was, finally, a goose, and last of all blancmange. Among the drinks were beer, vodka and sherry. The only bottle of champagne was standing beside the general, which obliged him to pour it out for himself and also for Akim Petrovitch, who did not venture at supper to officiate on his own initiative. The other guests had to drink the toasts in Caucasian wine or anything else they could get. The table was made up of several tables put together, among them even a cardtable. It was covered with many tablecloths, amongst them one coloured Yaroslav cloth; the gentlemen sat alternately with the ladies. Pseldonimov's mother would not sit down to the table; she bustled about and supervised. But another sinister female figure, who had not shown herself till then, appeared on the scene, wearing a reddish silk dress, with a very high cap on her head and a bandage round her face for toothache. It appeared that this was the bride's mother, who had at last consented to emerge from a back room for supper. She had refused to appear till then owing to her implacable hostility to Pseldonimov's mother, but to that we will refer later. This lady looked spitefully, even sarcastically, at the general, and evidently did not wish to be presented to him. To Ivan Ilyitch this figure appeared suspicious in the extreme. But apart from her, several other persons were suspicious and inspired involuntary apprehension and uneasiness. It even seemed that they were in some sort of plot together against Ivan Ilyitch. At any rate it seemed so to him, and throughout the whole supper he became more and more convinced of it. A gentleman with a beard, some sort of free artist, was particularly sinister; he even looked at Ivan Ilyitch several times, and then turning to his neighbour, whispered something. Another person present was unmistakably drunk, but yet, from certain signs, was to be regarded with suspicion. The medical student, too, gave rise to unpleasant expectations. Even the officer himself was not quite to be depended on. But the young man on the comic paper was blazing with hatred, he lolled in his chair, he looked so haughty and conceited, he snorted so aggressively! And though the rest of the guests took absolutely no notice of the young journalist, who had contributed only four wretched poems to the *Firebrand* , and had consequently become a Liberal and evidently, indeed, disliked him, yet when a pellet of bread aimed in his direction fell near Ivan Ilyitch, he was ready to stake his head that it had been thrown by no other than the young man in question.

All this, of course, had a pitiable effect on him.

Another observation was particularly unpleasant. Ivan Ilyitch became aware that he was beginning to articulate indistinctly and with difficulty, that he was longing to say a great deal, but that his tongue refused to obey him. And then he suddenly seemed to forget himself, and worst of all he would suddenly burst into a loud guffaw of laughter, *à propos* of nothing. This inclination quickly passed off after a glass of champagne which Ivan Ilyitch had not meant to drink, though he had poured it out and suddenly drunk it quite by accident. After that glass he felt at once almost inclined to cry. He felt that he was sinking into a most peculiar state of sentimentality; he began to be again filled with love, he loved every one, even Pseldonimov, even the young man on the comic paper. He suddenly longed to embrace all of them, to forget everything and to be reconciled. What is more, to tell them everything openly, all, all; that is, to tell them what a good, nice man he was, with what wonderful talents. What services he would do for his country, how good he was at entertaining the fair sex, and above all, how progressive he was, how humanely ready he was to be indulgent to all, to the very lowest; and finally in conclusion to tell them frankly all the motives that had impelled him to turn up at Pseldonimov's uninvited, to drink two bottles of champagne and to make him happy with his presence.

"The truth, the holy truth and candour before all things! I will capture them by candour. They will believe me, I see it clearly; they actually look at me with hostility, but when I tell them all I shall conquer them completely. They will fill their glasses and drink my health with shouts. The officer will break his glass on his spur. Perhaps they will even shout hurrah! Even if they want to toss me after the Hussar fashion I will not oppose them, and indeed it would be very jolly! I will kiss the bride on her forehead; she is charming. Akim Petrovitch is a very nice man, too. Pseldonimov will improve, of course, later on. He will acquire, so to speak, a society polish.... And although, of course, the younger generation has not that delicacy of feeling, yet...yet I will talk to them about the contemporary significance of Russia among the European States. I will refer to the peasant question, too; yes, and...and they will all like me and I shall leave with glory!..."

These dreams were, of course, extremely agreeable, but what was unpleasant was that in the midst of these roseate anticipations, Ivan Ilyitch suddenly discovered in himself another unexpected propensity, that was to spit. Anyway saliva began running from his mouth apart from any will of his own. He observed this on Akim Petrovitch, whose cheek he spluttered upon and who sat not daring to wipe it off from respectfulness. Ivan Ilyitch took his dinner napkin and wiped it himself, but this immediately struck him himself as so incongruous, so opposed to all common sense, that he sank into silence and began wondering. Though Akim Petrovitch emptied his glass, yet he sat as though he were scalded. Ivan Ilyitch reflected now that he had for almost a quarter of an hour been talking to him about some most interesting subject, but that Akim Petrovitch had not only seemed embarrassed as he listened, but positively frightened. Pseldonimov, who was sitting one chair away from him, also craned his neck towards him, and bending his head sideways, listened to him with the most unpleasant air. He actually seemed to be keeping a watch on him. Turning his eyes upon the rest of the company, he saw that many were looking straight at him and laughing. But what was strangest of all was, that he was not in the least embarrassed by it; on the contrary, he sipped his glass again and suddenly began speaking so that all could hear:

"I was saying just now," he began as loudly as possible, "I was saying just now, ladies and gentlemen, to Akim Petrovitch, that Russia...yes, Russia...in short, you understand, that I mean to s-s-say...Russia is living, it is my profound conviction, through a period of hu-hu-manity...."

"Hu-hu-manity ..," was heard at the other end of the table.

"Hu-hu...."

"Tu-tu!"

Ivan Ilyitch stopped. Pseldonimov got up from his chair and began trying to see who had shouted. Akim Petrovitch stealthily shook his head, as though admonishing the guests. Ivan Ilyitch saw this distinctly, but in his confusion said nothing.

"Humanity!" he continued obstinately; "and this evening...and only this evening I said to Stepan Niki-ki-forovitch...yes...that...that the regeneration, so to speak, of things...."

"Your Excellency!" was heard a loud exclamation at the other end of the table.

"What is your pleasure?" answered Ivan Ilyitch, pulled up short and trying to distinguish who had called to him.

"Nothing at all, your Excellency. I was carried away, continue! Con-ti-nue!" the voice was heard again.

Ivan Ilyitch felt upset.

"The regeneration, so to speak, of those same things."

"Your Excellency!" the voice shouted again.

"What do you want?"

"How do you do!"

This time Ivan Ilyitch could not restrain himself. He broke off his speech and turned to the assailant who had disturbed the general harmony. He was a very young lad, still at school, who had taken more than a drop too much, and was an object of great suspicion to the general. He had been shouting for a long time past, and had even broken a glass and two plates, maintaining that this was the proper thing to do at a wedding. At the moment when Ivan Ilyitch turned towards him, the officer was beginning to pitch into the noisy youngster.

"What are you about? Why are you yelling? We shall turn you out, that's what we shall do."

"I don't mean you, your Excellency, I don't mean you. Continue!" cried the hilarious schoolboy, lolling back in his chair. "Continue, I am listening, and am very, ve-ry, ve-ry much pleased with you! Praiseworthy, praiseworthy!"

"The wretched boy is drunk," said Pseldonimov in a whisper.

"I see that he is drunk, but...."

"I was just telling a very amusing anecdote, your Excellency!" began the officer, "about a lieutenant in our company who was talking just like that to his superior officers; so this young man is imitating him now. To every word of his superior officers he said 'praiseworthy, praiseworthy!' He was turned out of the army ten years ago on account of it."

"Wha-at lieutenant was that?"

"In our company, your Excellency, he went out of his mind over the word praiseworthy. At first they tried gentle methods, then they put him under arrest.... His commanding officer admonished him in the most fatherly way, and he answered, 'praiseworthy, praiseworthy!' And strange to say, the officer was a fine-looking man, over six feet. They meant to court-martial him, but then they perceived that he was mad."

"So...a schoolboy. A schoolboy's prank need not be taken seriously. For my part I am ready to overlook it...."

"They held a medical inquiry, your Excellency."

"Upon my word, but he was alive, wasn't he?"

"What! Did they dissect him?"

A loud and almost universal roar of laughter resounded among the guests, who had till then behaved with decorum. Ivan Ilyitch was furious.

"Ladies and gentlemen!" he shouted, at first scarcely stammering, "I am fully capable of apprehending that a man is not dissected alive. I imagined that in his derangement he had ceased to be alive...that is, that he had died...that is, I mean to say...that you don't like me... and yet I like you all...Yes, I like Por...Porfiry...I am lowering myself by speaking like this...."

At that moment Ivan Ilyitch spluttered so that a great dab of saliva flew on to the tablecloth in a most conspicuous place. Pseldonimov flew to wipe it off with a table-napkin. This last disaster crushed him completely.

"My friends, this is too much," he cried in despair.

"The man is drunk, your Excellency," Pseldonimov prompted him again.

"Porfiry, I see that you...all...yes! I say that I hope...yes, I call upon you all to tell me in what way have I lowered myself?"

Ivan Ilyitch was almost crying.

"Your Excellency, good heavens!"

"Porfiry, I appeal to you.... Tell me, when I came...yes...yes, to your wedding, I had an object. I was aiming at moral elevation.... I wanted it to be felt.... I appeal to all: am I greatly lowered in your eyes or not?"

A deathlike silence. That was just it, a deathlike silence, and to such a downright question. "They might at least shout at this minute!" flashed through his Excellency's head. But the guests only looked at one another. Akim Petrovitch sat more dead than alive, while Pseldonimov, numb with terror, was repeating to himself the awful question which had occurred to him more than once already.

"What shall I have to pay for all this tomorrow?"

At this point the young man on the comic paper, who was very drunk but who had hitherto sat in morose silence, addressed Ivan Ilyitch directly, and with flashing eyes began answering in the name of the whole company.

"Yes," he said in a loud voice, "yes, you have lowered yourself. Yes, you are a reactionary... re-ac-tionary!"

"Young man, you are forgetting yourself! To whom are you speaking, so to express it?" Ivan Ilyitch cried furiously, jumping up from his seat again.

"To you; and secondly, I am not a young man.... You've come to give yourself airs and try to win popularity."

"Pseldonimov, what does this mean?" cried Ivan Ilyitch.

But Pseldonimov was reduced to such horror that he stood still like a post and was utterly at a loss what to do. The guests, too, sat mute in their seats. All but the artist and the schoolboy, who applauded and shouted, "Bravo, bravo!"

The young man on the comic paper went on shouting with unrestrained violence:

"Yes, you came to show off your humanity! You've hindered the enjoyment of every one. You've been drinking champagne without thinking that it is beyond the means of a clerk at ten roubles a month. And I suspect that you are one of those high officials who are a little too fond of the young wives of their clerks! What is more, I am convinced that you support State monopolies.... Yes, yes, yes!"

"Pseldonimov, Pseldonimov," shouted Ivan Ilyitch, holding out his hands to him. He felt that every word uttered by the comic young man was a fresh dagger at his heart.

"Directly, your Excellency; please do not disturb yourself!" Pseldonimov cried energetically, rushing up to the comic young man, seizing him by the collar and dragging him away from the table. Such physical strength could indeed not have been expected from the weakly looking Pseldonimov. But the comic young man was very drunk, while Pseldonimov was perfectly sober. Then he gave him two or three cuffs in the back, and thrust him out of the door.

"You are all scoundrels!" roared the young man of the comic paper. "I will caricature you all tomorrow in the *Firebrand* ."

They all leapt up from their seats.

"Your Excellency, your Excellency!" cried Pseldonimov, his mother and several others, crowding round the general; "your Excellency, do not be disturbed!"

"No, no," cried the general, "I am annihilated.... I came...I meant to bless you, so to speak. And this is how I am paid, for everything, everything!..."

He sank on to a chair as though unconscious, laid both his arms on the table, and bowed his head over them, straight into a plate of blancmange. There is no need to describe the general horror. A minute later he got up, evidently meaning to go out, gave a lurch, stumbled against the leg of a chair, fell full length on the floor and snored....

This is what is apt to happen to men who don't drink when they accidentally take a glass too much. They preserve their consciousness to the last point, to the last minute, and then fall to the ground as though struck down. Ivan Ilyitch lay on the floor absolutely unconscious. Pseldonimov clutched at his hair and sat as though petrified in that position. The guests made haste to depart, commenting each in his own way on the incident. It was about three o'clock in the morning.

The worst of it was that Pseldonimov's circumstances were far worse than could have been imagined, in spite of the unattractiveness of his present surroundings. And while Ivan Ilyitch is lying on the floor and Pseldonimov is standing over him tearing his hair in despair, we will break off the thread of our story and say a few explanatory words about Porfiry Petrovitch Pseldonimov.

Not more than a month before his wedding he was in a state of hopeless destitution. He came from a province where his father had served in some department and where he had died while awaiting his trial on some charge. When five months before his wedding, Pseldonimov, who had been in hopeless misery in Petersburg for a whole year before, got his berth at ten roubles a month, he revived both physically and mentally, but he was soon crushed by circumstances again. There were only two Pseldonimovs left in the world, himself and his mother, who had left the province after her husband's death. The mother and son barely existed in the freezing cold, and sustained life on the most dubious substances. There were days when Pseldonimov himself went with a jug to the Fontanka for water to drink. When he got his place he succeeded in settling with his mother in a "corner." She took in washing, while for four months he scraped together every farthing to get himself boots and an overcoat. And what troubles he had to endure at his office; his superiors approached him with the question: "How long was it since he had had a bath?" There was a rumour about him that under the collar of his uniform there were nests of bugs. But Pseldonimov was a man of strong character. On the surface he was mild and meek; he had the merest smattering of education, he was practically never heard to talk of anything. I do not know for certain whether he thought, made plans and theories, had dreams. But on the other hand there was being formed within him an instinctive, furtive, unconscious determination to fight his way out of his wretched circumstances. He had the persistence of an ant. Destroy an ants' nest, and they will begin at once re-erecting it; destroy it again, and they will begin again without wearying. He was a constructive house-building animal. One could see from his brow that he would make his way, would build his nest, and perhaps even save for a rainy day. His mother was the only creature in the world who loved him, and she loved him beyond everything. She was a woman of resolute character, hardworking and indefatigable, and at the same time goodnatured. So perhaps they might have lived in their corner for five or six years till their circumstances changed, if they had not come across the retired titular councillor Mlekopitaev, who had been a clerk in the treasury and had served at one time in the provinces, but had latterly settled in Petersburg and had established himself there with his family. He knew Pseldonimov, and had at one time been under some obligation to his father. He had a little money, not a large sum, of course, but there it was; how much it was no one knew, not his wife, nor his elder daughter, nor his relations. He had two daughters, and as he was an awful bully, a drunkard, a domestic tyrant, and in addition to that an invalid, he took it into his head one day to marry one of his daughters to Pseldonimov: "I knew his father," he would say, "he was a good fellow and his son will be a good fellow." Mlekopitaev did exactly as he liked, his word was law. He was a very queer bully. For the most part he spent his time sitting in an armchair, having lost the use of his legs from some disease which did not, however, prevent him from drinking vodka. For days together he would be drinking and swearing. He was an ill-natured man. He always wanted to have some one whom he could be continually tormenting. And for that purpose he kept several distant relations: his sister, a sickly and peevish woman; two of his wife's sisters, also ill-natured and very free with their tongues, and his old aunt, who had through some accident a broken rib; he kept another dependent also, a Russianised German, for the sake of her talent for entertaining him with stories from the *Arabian Nights*. His sole gratification consisted in jeering at all these unfortunate women and abusing them every minute with all his energies; though the latter, not excepting his wife, who had been born with toothache, dared not utter a word in his presence. He set them at loggerheads at one another, inventing and fostering spiteful backbiting and dissensions among them, and then laughed and rejoiced seeing how they were ready to tear one another to pieces. He was very much delighted when his elder daughter, who had lived in great poverty for ten years with her husband, an officer of some sort, and was at last left a widow, came to live with him with three little sickly children. He could not endure her children, but as her arrival had increased the material upon which he could work his daily experiments, the old man was very much pleased. All these ill-natured women and sickly children, together with their tormentor, were crowded together in a wooden house on Petersburg Side, and did not get enough to eat because the old man was stingy and gave out to them money a farthing at a time, though he did not grudge himself vodka; they did not get enough sleep because the old man suffered from sleeplessness and insisted on being amused. In short, they all were in misery and cursed their fate. It was at that time that Mlekopitaev's eye fell upon Pseldonimov. He was struck by his long nose and submissive air. His weakly and unprepossessing younger daughter had just reached the age of seventeen. Though she had at one time attended a German school, she had acquired scarcely anything but the alphabet. Then she grew up rickety and anæmic in fear of her crippled drunken father's crutch, in a Bedlam of domestic backbiting, eavesdropping and scolding. She had never had any friends or any brains. She had for a long time been eager to be married. In company she sat mute, but at home with her mother and the women of the household she was spiteful and cantankerous. She was particularly fond of pinching and smacking her sister's children, telling tales of their pilfering bread and sugar, and this led to endless and implacable strife with her elder sister. Her old father himself offered her to Pseldonimov. Miserable as the latter's position was, he yet asked for a little time to consider. His mother and he hesitated for a long time. But with the young lady there was to come as dowry a house, and though it was a nasty little wooden house of one storey, yet it was property of a kind. Moreover, they would give with her four hundred roubles, and how long it would take him to save it up himself! "What am I taking the man into my house for?" shouted the drunken bully. "In the first place because you are all females, and I am sick of female society. I want Pseldonimov, too, to dance to my piping. For I am his benefactor. And in the second place I am doing it because you are all cross and don't want it, so I'll do it to spite you. What I have said, I have said! And you beat her, Porfiry, when she is your wife; she has been possessed of seven devils ever since she was born. You beat them out of her, and I'll get the stick ready."

Pseldonimov made no answer, but he was already decided. Before the wedding his mother and he were taken into the house, washed, clothed, provided with boots and money for the wedding. The old man took them under his protection possibly just because the whole family was prejudiced against them. He positively liked Pseldonimov's mother, so that he actually restrained himself and did not jeer at her. On the other hand, he made Pseldonimov dance the Cossack dance a week before the wedding.

"Well, that's enough. I only wanted to see whether you remembered your position before me or not," he said at the end of the dance. He allowed just enough money for the wedding, with nothing to spare, and invited all his relations and acquaintances. On Pseldonimov's side there was no one but the young man who wrote for the *Firebrand*, and Akim Petrovitch, the guest of honour. Pseldonimov was perfectly aware that his bride cherished an aversion for him, and that she was set upon marrying the officer instead of him. But he put up with everything, he had made a compact with his mother to do so. The old father had been drunk and abusive and foul-tongued the whole of the wedding day and during the party in the evening. The whole family took refuge in the back rooms and were crowded there to suffocation. The front rooms were devoted to the dance and the supper. At last when the old man fell asleep dead drunk at eleven o'clock, the bride's mother, who had been particularly displeased with Pseldonimov's mother that day, made up her mind to lay aside her wrath, become gracious and join the company. Ivan Ilyitch's arrival had turned everything upside down. Madame Mlekopitaev was overcome with embarrassment, and began grumbling that she had not been told that the general had been invited. She was assured that he had come uninvited, but was so stupid as to refuse to believe it. Champagne had to be got. Pseldonimov's mother had only one rouble, while Pseldonimov himself had not one farthing. He had to grovel before his ill-natured mother-in-law, to beg for the money for one bottle and then for another. They pleaded for the sake of his future position in the service, for his career, they tried to persuade her. She did at last give from her own purse, but she forced Pseldonimov to swallow such a cupful of gall and bitterness that more than once he ran into the room where the nuptial couch had been prepared, and madly clutching at his hair and trembling all over with impotent rage, he buried his head in the bed destined for the joys of paradise. No, indeed, Ivan Ilyitch had no notion of the price paid for the two bottles of Jackson he had drunk that evening. What was the horror, the misery and even the despair of Pseldonimov when Ivan Ilyitch's visit ended in this unexpected way. He had a prospect again of no end of misery, and perhaps a night of tears and outcries from his peevish bride, and upbraidings from her unreasonable relations. Even apart from this his head ached already, and there was dizziness and mist before his eyes. And here Ivan Ilyitch needed looking after, at three o'clock at night he had to hunt for a doctor or a carriage to take him home, and a carriage it must be, for it would be impossible to let an ordinary cabby take him home in that condition. And where could he get the money even for a carriage? Madame Mlekopitaev, furious that the general had not addressed two words to her, and had not even looked at her at supper, declared that she had not a farthing. Possibly she really had not a farthing. Where could he get it? What was he to do? Yes, indeed, he had good cause to tear his hair.

Meanwhile Ivan Ilyitch was moved to a little leather sofa that stood in the dining-room. While they were clearing the tables and putting them away, Pseldonimov was rushing all over the place to borrow money, he even tried to get it from the servants, but it appeared that nobody had any. He even ventured to trouble Akim Petrovitch who had stayed after the other guests. But goodnatured as he was, the latter was reduced to such bewilderment and even alarm at the mention of money that he uttered the most unexpected and foolish phrases:

"Another time, with pleasure," he muttered, "but now...you really must excuse me...."

And taking his cap, he ran as fast as he could out of the house. Only the goodnatured youth who had talked about the dream book was any use at all; and even that came to nothing. He, too, stayed after the others, showing genuine sympathy with Pseldonimov's misfortunes. At last Pseldonimov, together with his mother and the young man, decided in consultation not to send for a doctor, but rather to fetch a carriage and take the invalid home, and meantime to try certain domestic remedies till the carriage arrived, such as moistening his temples and his head with cold water, putting ice on his head, and so on. Pseldonimov's mother undertook this task. The friendly youth flew off in search of a carriage. As there were not even ordinary cabs to be found on the Petersburg Side at that hour, he went off to some livery stables at a distance to wake up the coachmen. They began bargaining, and declared that five roubles would be little to ask for a carriage at that time of night. They agreed to come, however, for three. When at last, just before five o'clock, the young man arrived at Pseldonimov's with the carriage, they had changed their minds. It appeared that Ivan Ilyitch, who was still unconscious, had become so seriously unwell, was moaning and tossing so terribly, that to move him and take him home in such a condition was impossible and actually unsafe. "What will it lead to next?" said Pseldonimov, utterly disheartened. What was to be done? A new problem arose: if the invalid remained in the house, where should he be moved and where could they put him? There were only two bedsteads in the house: one large double bed in which old Mlekopitaev and his wife slept, and another double bed of imitation walnut which had just been purchased and was destined for the newly married couple. All the other inhabitants of the house slept on the floor side by side on feather beds, for the most part in bad condition and stuffy, anything but presentable in fact, and even of these the supply was insufficient; there was not one to spare. Where could the invalid be put? A feather bed might perhaps have been found — it might in the last resort have been pulled from under some one, but where and on what could a bed have been made up? It seemed that the bed must be made up in the drawing-room, for that room was the furthest from the bosom of the family and had a door into the passage. But on what could the bed be made? Surely not upon chairs. We all know that beds can only be made up on chairs for schoolboys when they come home for the week end, and it would be terribly lacking in respect to make up a bed in that way for a personage like Ivan Ilyitch. What would be said next morning when he found himself lying on chairs? Pseldonimov would not hear of that. The only alternative was to put him on the bridal couch. This bridal couch, as we have mentioned already, was in a little room that opened out of the dining-room, on the bedstead was a double mattress actually newly bought first-hand, clean sheets, four pillows in pink calico covered with frilled muslin cases. The quilt was of pink satin, and it was quilted in patterns. Muslin curtains hung down from a golden ring overhead, in fact it was all just as it should be, and the guests who had all visited the bridal chamber had admired the decoration of it; though the bride could not endure Pseldonimov, she had several times in the course of the evening run in to have a look at it on the sly. What was her indignation, her wrath, when she learned that they meant to move an invalid, suffering from something not unlike a mild attack of cholera, to her bridal couch! The bride's mother took her part, broke into abuse and vowed she would complain to her husband next day, but Pseldonimov asserted himself and insisted: Ivan Ilyitch was moved into the bridal chamber, and a bed was made up on chairs for the young people. The bride whimpered, would have liked to pinch him, but dared not disobey; her papa had a crutch with which she was very familiar, and she knew that her papa would call her to account next day. To console her they carried the pink satin quilt and the pillows in muslin cases into the drawing-room. At that moment the youth arrived with the carriage, and was horribly alarmed that the carriage was not wanted. He was left to pay for it himself, and he never had as much as a ten-kopeck piece. Pseldonimov explained that he was utterly bankrupt. They tried to parley with the driver. But he began to be noisy and even to batter on the shutters. How it ended I don't know exactly. I believe the youth was carried off to Peski by way of a hostage to Fourth Rozhdensky Street, where he hoped to rouse a student who was spending the night at a friend's, and to try whether he had any money. It was going on for six o'clock in the morning when the young people were left alone and shut up in the drawing-room. Pseldonimov's mother spent the whole night by the bedside of the sufferer. She installed herself on a rug on the floor and covered herself with an old coat, but could not sleep because she had to get up every minute: Ivan Ilyitch had a terrible attack of colic. Madame Pseldonimov, a woman of courage and greatness of soul, undressed him with her own hands, took off all his things, looked after him as if he were her own son, and spent the whole night carrying basins, etc., from the bedroom across the passage and bringing them back again empty. And yet the misfortunes of that night were not yet over.

Not more than ten minutes after the young people had been shut up alone in the drawing-room, a piercing shriek was suddenly heard, not a cry of joy, but a shriek of the most sinister kind. The screams were followed by a noise, a crash, as though of the falling of chairs, and instantly there burst into the still dark room a perfect crowd of exclaiming and frightened women, attired in every kind of *déshabillé*. These women were the bride's mother, her elder sister, abandoning for the moment the sick children, and her three aunts, even the one with a broken rib dragged herself in. Even the cook was there, and the German lady who told stories, whose own feather bed, the best in the house, and her only property, had been forcibly dragged from under her for the young couple, trailed in together with the others. All these respectable and sharp-eyed ladies had, a quarter of an hour before, made their way on tiptoe from the kitchen across the passage, and were listening in the anteroom, devoured by unaccountable curiosity. Meanwhile some one lighted a candle, and a surprising spectacle met the eyes of all. The chairs supporting the broad feather bed only at the sides had parted under the weight, and the feather bed had fallen between them on the floor. The bride was sobbing with anger, this time she was mortally offended. Pseldonimov, morally shattered, stood like a criminal caught in a crime. He did not even attempt to defend himself. Shrieks and exclamations sounded on all sides. Pseldonimov's mother ran up at the noise, but the bride's mamma on this occasion got the upper hand. She began by showering strange and for the most part quite undeserved reproaches, such as: "A nice husband you are, after this. What are you good for after such a disgrace?" and so on; and at last carried her daughter away from her husband, undertaking to bear the full responsibility for doing so with her ferocious husband, who would demand an explanation. All the others followed her out exclaiming and shaking their heads. No one remained with Pseldonimov except his mother, who tried to comfort him. But he sent her away at once.

He was beyond consolation. He made his way to the sofa and sat down in the most gloomy confusion of mind just as he was, barefooted and in nothing but his night attire. His thoughts whirled in a tangled criss-cross in his mind. At times he mechanically looked about the room where only a little while ago the dancers had been whirling madly, and in which the cigarette smoke still lingered. Cigarette ends and sweetmeat papers still littered the slopped and dirty floor. The wreck of the nuptial couch and the overturned chairs bore witness to the transitoriness of the fondest and surest earthly hopes and dreams. He sat like this almost an hour. The most oppressive thoughts kept coming into his mind, such as the doubt: What was in store for him in the office now? He recognised with painful clearness that he would have, at all costs, to exchange into another department; that he could not possibly remain where he was after all that had happened that evening. He thought, too, of Mlekopitaev, who would probably make him dance the Cossack dance next day to test his meekness. He reflected, too, that though Mlekopitaev had given fifty roubles for the wedding festivities, every farthing of which had been spent, he had not thought of giving him the four hundred roubles yet, no mention had been made of it, in fact. And, indeed, even the house had not been formally made over to him. He thought, too, of his wife who had left him at the most critical moment of his life, of the tall officer who had dropped on one knee before her. He had noticed that already; he thought of the seven devils which according to the testimony of her own father were in possession of his wife, and of the crutch in readiness to drive them out.... Of course he felt equal to bearing a great deal, but destiny had let loose such surprises upon him that he might well have doubts of his fortitude. So Pseldonimov mused dolefully. Meanwhile the candle end was going out, its fading light, falling straight upon Pseldonimov's profile, threw a colossal shadow of it on the wall, with a drawn-out neck, a hooked nose, and with two tufts of hair sticking out on his forehead and the back of his head. At last, when the air was growing cool with the chill of early morning, he got up, frozen and spiritually numb, crawled to the feather bed that was lying between the chairs, and without rearranging anything, without putting out the candle end, without even laying the pillow under his head, fell into a leaden, deathlike sleep, such as the sleep of men condemned to flogging on the morrow must be.

On the other hand, what could be compared with the agonising night spent by Ivan Ilyitch Pralinsky on the bridal couch of the unlucky Pseldonimov! For some time, headache, vomiting and other most unpleasant symptoms did not leave him for one second. He was in the torments of hell. The faint glimpses of consciousness that visited his brain, lighted up such an abyss of horrors, such gloomy and revolting pictures, that it would have been better for him not to have returned to consciousness. Everything was still in a turmoil in his mind, however. He recognised Pseldonimov's mother, for instance, heard her gentle admonitions, such as: "Be patient, my dear; be patient, good sir, it won't be so bad presently." He recognised her, but could give no logical explanation of her presence beside him. Revolting phantoms haunted him, most frequently of all he was haunted by Semyon Ivanitch; but looking more intently, he saw that it was not Semyon Ivanitch but Pseldonimov's nose. He had visions, too, of the free-and-easy artist, and the officer and the old lady with her face tied up. What interested him most of all was the gilt ring which hung over his head, through which the curtains hung. He could distinguish it distinctly in the dim light of the candle end which lighted up the room, and he kept wondering inwardly: What was the object of that ring, why was it there, what did it mean? He questioned the old lady several times about it, but apparently did not say what he meant; and she evidently did not understand it, however much he struggled to explain. At last by morning the symptoms had ceased and he fell into a sleep, a sound sleep without dreams. He slept about an hour, and when he woke he was almost completely conscious, with an insufferable headache, and a disgusting taste in his mouth and on his tongue, which seemed turned into a piece of cloth. He sat up in the bed, looked about him, and pondered. The pale light of morning peeping through the cracks of the shutters in a narrow streak, quivered on the wall. It was about seven o'clock in the morning. But when Ivan Ilyitch suddenly grasped the position and recalled all that had happened to him since the evening; when he remembered all his adventures at supper, the failure of his magnanimous action, his speech at table; when he realised all at once with horrifying clearness all that might come of this now, all that people would say and think of him; when he looked round and saw to what a mournful and hideous condition he had reduced the peaceful bridal couch of his clerk — oh, then such deadly shame, such agony overwhelmed him, that he uttered a shriek, hid his face in his hands and fell back on the pillow in despair. A minute later he jumped out of bed, saw his clothes carefully folded and brushed on a chair beside him, and seizing them, and as quickly as he could, in desperate haste began putting them on, looking round and seeming terribly frightened at something. On another chair close by lay his greatcoat and fur cap, and his yellow gloves were in his cap. He meant to steal away secretly. But suddenly the door opened and the elder Madame Pseldonimov walked in with an earthenware jug and basin. A towel was hanging over her shoulder. She set down the jug, and without further conversation told him that he must wash.

"Come, my good sir, wash; you can't go without washing...."

And at that instant Ivan Ilyitch recognised that if there was one being in the whole world whom he need not fear, and before whom he need not feel ashamed, it was that old lady. He washed. And long afterwards, at painful moments of his life, he recalled among other pangs of remorse all the circumstances of that waking, and that earthenware basin, and the china jug filled with cold water in which there were still floating icicles, and the oval cake of soap at fifteen kopecks, in pink paper with letters embossed on it, evidently bought for the bridal pair though it fell to Ivan Ilyitch to use it, and the old lady with the linen towel over her left shoulder. The cold water refreshed him, he dried his face, and without even thanking his sister of mercy, he snatched up his hat, flung over his shoulders the coat handed to him by Pseldonimov, and crossing the passage and the kitchen where the cat was already mewing, and the cook sitting up in her bed staring after him with greedy curiosity, ran out into the yard, into the street, and threw himself into the first sledge he came across. It was a frosty morning. A chilly yellow fog still hid the house and everything. Ivan Ilyitch turned up his collar. He thought that every one was looking at him, that they were all recognising him, all....

For eight days he did not leave the house or show himself at the office. He was ill, wretchedly ill, but more morally than physically. He lived through a perfect hell in those days, and they must have been reckoned to his account in the other world. There were moments when he thought of becoming a monk and entering a monastery. There really were. His imagination, indeed, took special excursions during that period. He pictured subdued subterranean singing, an open coffin, living in a solitary cell, forests and caves; but when he came to himself he recognised almost at once that all this was dreadful nonsense and exaggeration, and was ashamed of this nonsense. Then began attacks of moral agony on the theme of his *existence manquée* . Then shame flamed up again in his soul, took complete possession of him at once, consumed him like fire and reopened his wounds. He shuddered as pictures of all sorts rose before his mind. What would people say about him, what would they think when he walked into his office? What a whisper would dog his steps for a whole year, ten years, his whole life! His story would go down to posterity. He sometimes fell into such dejection that he was ready to go straight off to Semyon Ivanovitch and ask for his forgiveness and friendship. He did not even justify himself, there was no limit to his blame of himself. He could find no extenuating circumstances, and was ashamed of trying to.

He had thoughts, too, of resigning his post at once and devoting himself to human happiness as a simple citizen, in solitude. In any case he would have completely to change his whole circle of acquaintances, and so thoroughly as to eradicate all memory of himself. Then the thought occurred to him that this, too, was nonsense, and that if he adopted greater severity with his subordinates it might all be set right. Then he began to feel hope and courage again. At last, at the expiration of eight days of hesitation and agonies, he felt that he could not endure to be in uncertainty any longer, and *un beau matin* he made up his mind to go to the office.

He had pictured a thousand times over his return to the office as he sat at home in misery. With horror and conviction he told himself that he would certainly hear behind him an ambiguous whisper, would see ambiguous faces, would intercept ominous smiles. What was his surprise when nothing of the sort happened. He was greeted with respect; he was met with bows; every one was grave; every one was busy. His heart was filled with joy as he made his way to his own room.

He set to work at once with the utmost gravity, he listened to some reports and explanations, settled doubtful points. He felt as though he had never explained knotty points and given his decisions so intelligently, so judiciously as that morning. He saw that they were satisfied with him, that they respected him, that he was treated with respect. The most thin-skinned sensitiveness could not have discovered anything.

At last Akim Petrovitch made his appearance with some document. The sight of him sent a stab to Ivan Ilyitch's heart, but only for an instant. He went into the business with Akim Petrovitch, talked with dignity, explained things, and showed him what was to be done. The only thing he noticed was that he avoided looking at Akim Petrovitch for any length of time, or rather Akim Petrovitch seemed afraid of catching his eye, but at last Akim Petrovitch had finished and began to collect his papers.

"And there is one other matter," he began as dryly as he could, "the clerk Pseldonimov's petition to be transferred to another department. His Excellency Semyon Ivanovitch Shipulenko has promised him a post. He begs your gracious assent, your Excellency."

"Oh, so he is being transferred," said Ivan Ilyitch, and he felt as though a heavy weight had rolled off his heart. He glanced at Akim Petrovitch, and at that instant their eyes met. "Certainly, I for my part...I will use," answered Ivan Ilyitch; "I am ready."

Akim Petrovitch evidently wanted to slip away as quickly as he could. But in a rush of generous feeling Ivan Ilyitch determined to speak out. Apparently some inspiration had come to him again.

"Tell him," he began, bending a candid glance full of profound meaning upon Akim Petrovitch, "tell Pseldonimov that I feel no ill-will, no, I do not!...That on the contrary I am ready to forget all that is past, to forget it all...."

But all at once Ivan Ilyitch broke off, looking with wonder at the strange behaviour of Akim Petrovitch, who suddenly seemed transformed from a sensible person into a fearful fool. Instead of listening and hearing Ivan Ilyitch to the end, he suddenly flushed crimson in the silliest way, began with positively unseemly haste making strange little bows, and at the same time edging towards the door. His whole appearance betrayed a desire to sink through the floor, or more accurately, to get back to his table as quickly as possible. Ivan Ilyitch, left alone, got up from his chair in confusion; he looked in the looking-glass without noticing his face.

"No, severity, severity and nothing but severity," he whispered almost unconsciously, and suddenly a vivid flush overspread his face. He felt suddenly more ashamed, more weighed down than he had been in the most insufferable moments of his eight days of tribulation. "I did break down!" he said to himself, and sank helplessly into his chair.

Lightning Source UK Ltd.
Milton Keynes UK
UKHW020937151221
395631UK00008B/2006

9 788027 333653